# I Did It!

by Mickey Daronco

"Can I hit it?" said Ron.
Ron did hit it.
It went and went.

"Can I pin it?" said Jan. Jan did not see it, but she did put the pin in.

"It is not hot," said Jan.
"I will have to zip up."

"Will a hat be in the red box?" said Jim.
"I will rip it and see."

"Look at me," said Pam.
"I will dip it in."

"Can I do it?" said Val.
"Can I fit it in?"

"Yes, I can," Val said.
"I did it!"